For Joe and Leo,
sweet dreams always – J.D

To my father, Dudley Reynolds, who first told me
about the Imperial Elephant, and to his grandchildren
and great-grandchildren, because he would want
them to know this story too – D.R.R.

The Elephant's Pillow copyright © Frances Lincoln Limited 2003
Text copyright © Diana Reynolds Roome 2003
Illustrations copyright © Jude Daly 2003
By arrangement with The Inkman, Cape Town, South Africa

First published in Great Britain in 2003 by
Frances Lincoln Limited, 4 Torriano Mews
Torriano Avenue, London NW5 2RZ

www.franceslincoln.com

British Library Cataloguing in Publication Data
available on request

ISBN 0-7112-1956-7

Set in Hiroshige

Printed in Singapore

3 5 7 9 8 6 4 2

THE ELEPHANT'S PILLOW

Diana Reynolds Roome

Illustrated by Jude Daly

FRANCES LINCOLN

L ong ago in the city of Peking,
   there lived a boy named
   Sing Lo.

His father was a rich merchant,
so he had everything he could want.

One morning Li, his rickshaw man,
arrived to take him for an outing.
Li knew every paving-stone of Peking
and had shown Sing Lo all the grand
sights. But Sing Lo wasn't satisfied.

"What is the greatest sight of all?"
he asked.

"Once, when I was little," said Li, panting as he ran,
"my father took me to see a grand parade. The Emperor
passed right by us on his elephant!"

"I wish to see this Imperial Elephant," demanded Sing Lo.

"When the old Emperor died," Li said sadly, "the elephant refused to carry anyone. People say that now he is a nasty-tempered beast."

Sing Lo thought hard.

"Maybe a present would cheer him up," he suggested.

"I've heard," said Li, "that the old Emperor used to give him special buns.
Let's visit my friend Wang Ching, the best baker in all Peking."

Off they sped to Bakers' Street. They stopped at a stall selling nothing but buns,
glazed with honey and sprinkled with poppy seeds.

"How many?" asked Wang Ching.

"All you have, " said Li. "The Imperial Elephant has waited a long time."

At last they arrived at a temple. A priest came out to greet them.

"I've come to see the Imperial Elephant," announced Sing Lo.

The priest looked worried.

"The elephant doesn't like visitors," he said. But he led Sing Lo
to a great, dark door covered in metal studs. From behind the door
came snuffling sounds. The ground shook a little as something
enormous stomped about inside.

"Be careful," muttered the priest. "Ever since
the old Emperor died, the elephant hasn't slept a wink."
He pulled open the door and walked quickly away.

Inside, in the dim light, Sing Lo could see a huge shape.

"O Imperial Elephant," called Sing Lo nervously.

"I have something for you."

The elephant did not move.

Sing Lo rustled the paper bag.
He stared, as one beady eye opened
and one leathery ear twitched.

"Your favourites," said Sing Lo,
edging away.

Slowly the great, grey trunk unfurled.
One bun disappeared, then another ...
and another ... until not a poppy seed
was left.

But the elephant stood shifting
back and forth uneasily.

"O Imperial Elephant, is there
something else?"

There was a low rumbly sound
as the elephant's trunk touched
Sing Lo's ear.

"The old Emperor used to give me
a bedtime drink."

"Wait here, " said Sing Lo.

Outside, the priest was waiting under a gingko tree.

"The elephant wants his bedtime drink," announced Sing Lo.

The priest looked surprised, but he bowed and walked back to the temple. Soon he came out holding an empty golden bowl.

"Honey above, ginger below, milk between," the priest said solemnly.

"What can he mean?" thought Sing Lo. He took the bowl and hurried back to the rickshaw. Li would know what to do. But Li was fast asleep. Sing Lo prodded him and tugged his pigtail, but Li would not wake up.

"I'll have to get it myself," said Sing Lo rather crossly. He'd never had to do anything for himself before now.

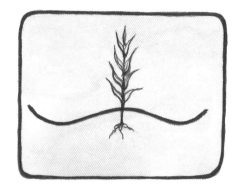

He gazed up at the gingko tree. Among the leaves, he caught sight of a wild bees' nest.

"Honey above!" he exclaimed. He inched up the trunk and pulled off a sticky chunk of honeycomb. But an angry bee followed him down.

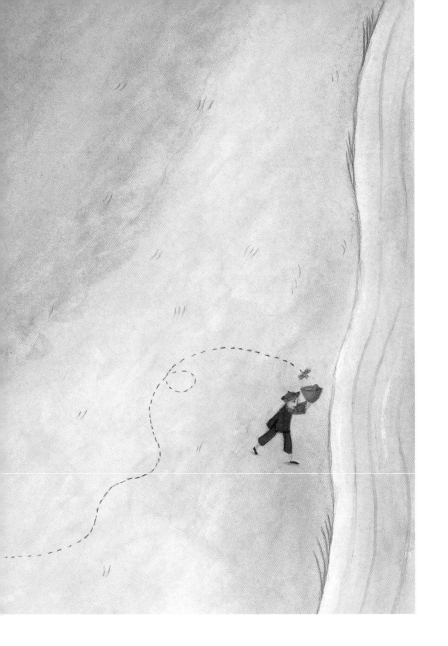

Sing Lo dashed towards the river, holding the bowl and the honey high.
As he pulled himself out of the water, he sniffed a delicious fragrance –
and there was the bee gathering nectar.

"Ginger below!" he cried, and dug down to pull up the ginger root.

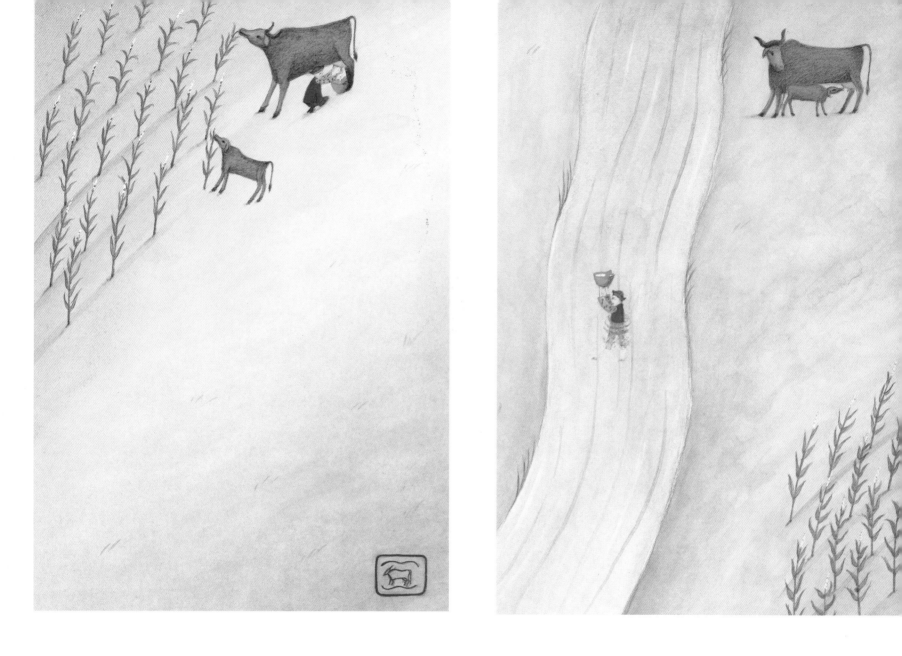

Munching contentedly on the patch of plants stood a buffalo and her calf.

"Milk between!" whispered Sing Lo triumphantly, and the buffalo hardly noticed when he helped himself. With honey, ginger and milk in the bowl, he waded back across the river.

Outside the elephant's stall, Sing Lo
stirred the drink. He pulled open
the great door and held out the bowl.

The elephant plopped in his trunk
and sucked – *thhssswpp!* He swung
his trunk up under his chin and shot
the drink into his mouth. Not a drop
was spilt.

Then he raised his trunk, almost
knocking Sing Lo off his feet.

"Still I cannot sleep!" he trumpeted.

"Why not?" asked Sing Lo.

"The Imperial Elephant cannot
sleep on straw!"

"What does the Imperial Elephant
sleep on?"

"The old Emperor gave me
a yellow pillow!"

"I'll be back," said Sing Lo quietly.

He dashed out to the rickshaw.

"Li," he said. "Take me to Silk Street!"

"My friend Ab Fat is the best silk merchant in all Peking," Li replied.
"Master could visit him tomorrow."

"The Imperial Elephant cannot wait," said Sing Lo. "Hurry!"

"Good day, Ab Fat," said Li, skidding to a stop. "My master needs
a yellow pillow – this big – with tassels. Have it ready by this afternoon."

When they arrived back at the temple, the sun was low in the sky.

From inside came mysterious sounds of chanting.

Sing Lo tiptoed into the stall.

"Close your eyes tightly," he whispered. He laid the pillow down on the straw.

"Behold, O Imperial Elephant!" he cried.

The elephant opened one eye and stared at the pillow. He felt it carefully with his trunk.

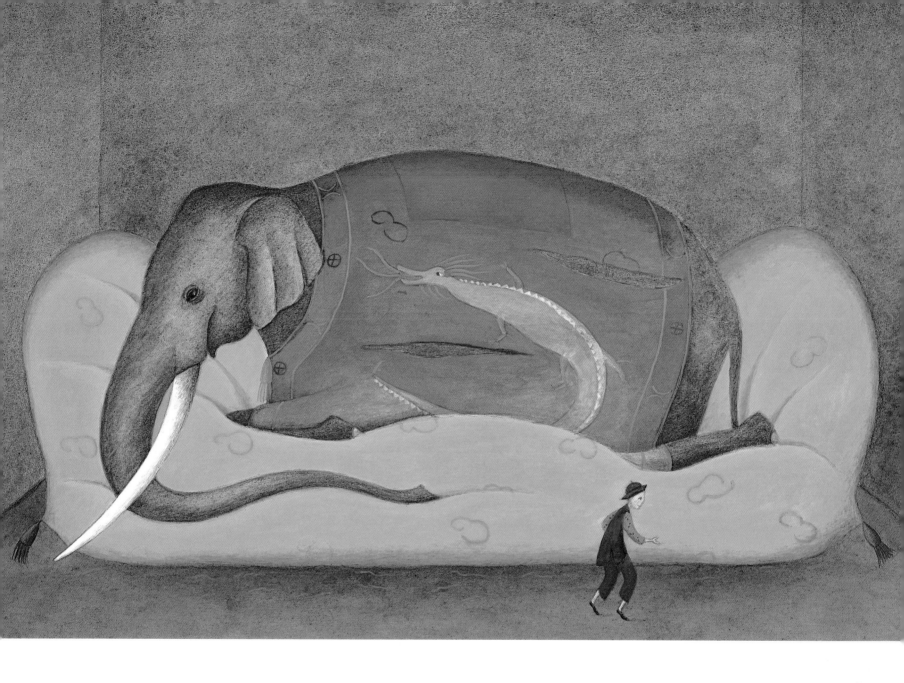

His back knees bent, his front knees folded. With a huge sigh, his head sank down.

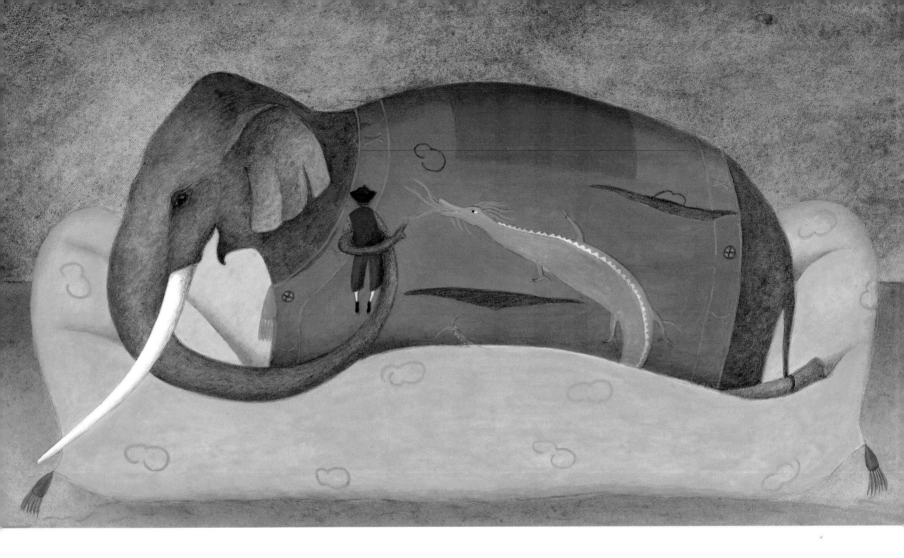

But suddenly he rumbled, "One more thing!"

"What could that be?" asked Sing Lo.

"The Emperor always scratched my neck, just behind my ear."

Sing Lo looked up and gasped. How would he reach?

"Up you come," said the elephant. He curled his trunk around
Sing Lo and lifted him off the ground. Sing Lo scrambled on to
the elephant's back.

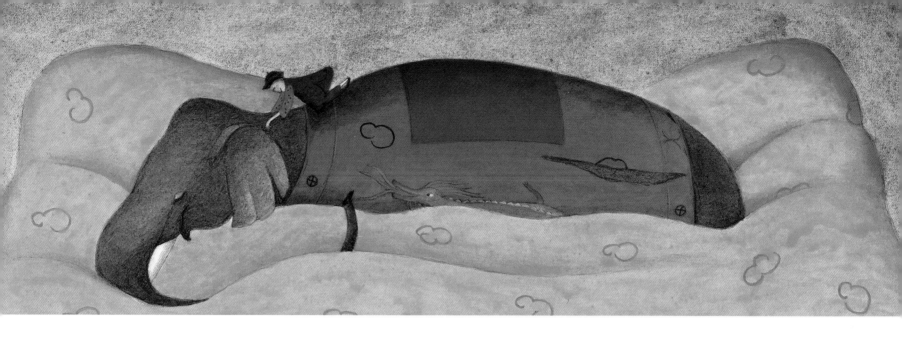

He stretched out his hand and scratched the gnarled neck.

Slowly the elephant's head started to sink down until it touched the pillow.

His eyes closed and his head sank deeper into the soft yellow silk. Soon a low
thrum of snoring joined the chanting from the temple.

Sing Lo smiled.

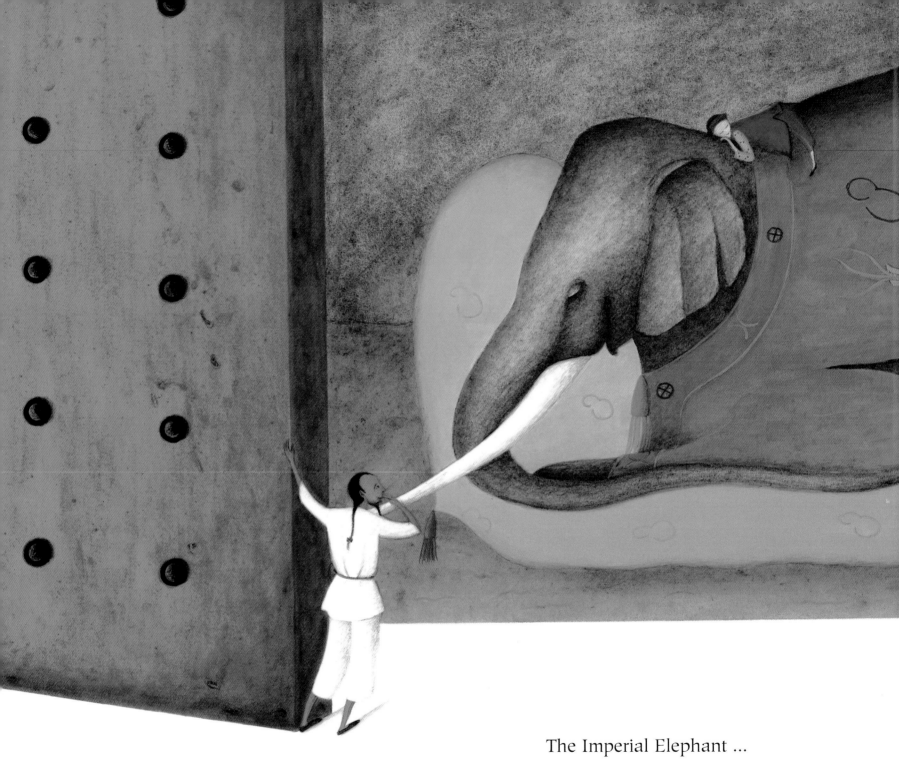

The Imperial Elephant ...

was fast asleep.